KT-385-363

Pippa Hoppytail's Rocky Road

Daisy Meadows

ORCHARD

Scramblepaws' Igloo

Grizelda's Lair

Littleleap Crossing Station

Fluffywhiskers Garden Station

Fluffywhiskers Garden

Fluffywhiskers Garden

Forest Halt Station

Forest Halt

Friendship Forest

Can you keep a secret? I thought you could!

Then I'll tell you about an enchanted wood.

It lies through the door in the old oak tree,

Let's go there now - just follow me!

We'll find adventure that never ends,

And meet the Magic Animal Friends!

Love,
Goldie the Cat

Contents

CHAPTER ONE

A Puzzling Letter

"Breakfast time!" called Lily Hart. Lily and her best friend, Jess Forester, were carrying buckets of feed out of the Helping Paw Wildlife Hospital.

The hospital was run by Lily's parents in a barn in their garden, and some of the patients were in pens outside, enjoying

 9

the spring sunshine. Jess and Lily adored animals, and loved helping to care for them.

Little guinea pig noses snuffled at their fence and, in another run, three baby squirrels scampered around excitedly. They were ready for breakfast!

Jess and Lily set to work. Soon, nearly all the bowls were filled with carrots, nuts or fresh green leaves.

"Just the rabbits left to feed now," said Lily, crossing the lawn. "They were feeling much better yesterday, so I bet they'll want a big breakfast!"

The girls walked over to the rabbit run, but when they got there – it was empty!

Jess gasped. "Where are they?"

They looked in the hutches. There was nothing but straw.

Then Lily found a hole in the side of the run. "Oh no!" she cried. "The rabbits have escaped!"

"Quick! Search the garden!" said Jess.

They split up. Lily looked in the flowerbeds, and Jess checked Mrs Hart's vegetable patch. Lily spotted the tips of two little ears behind a clump of daffodils, but when she reached the flowers the rabbit had vanished.

Jess saw a white tail bobbing behind a gooseberry bush. She crept over, but the bunny scampered away.

12

"If only the rabbits could talk, like they can in Friendship Forest," said Lily. "Then we could call after them, and try and find them."

Friendship Forest was the two best friends' amazing secret. It was a magical world where the animals lived in little cottages or on boats – even in a windmill! The girls' special friend, Goldie the cat, often took them to the forest, where they'd had some truly fantastic adventures.

The girls put bowls of lettuce beside the rabbit run. "That might tempt them out of hiding," said Lily.

Jess added some dandelion buds. "They love these."

But Lily wasn't watching. She had seen a movement among the blackcurrant bushes. At first she thought it was an escaped bunny, but then she saw a flash of golden fur. Out bounded a beautiful green-eyed cat.

"Goldie!" she cried.

The cat ran to the girls and curled around their legs, purring.

"She's come to take us to Friendship Forest!" Jess said.

Goldie darted towards Brightley Stream,at the bottom of the garden. Then she bounded across the stepping stones to the far bank, and into Brightley Meadow.

Jess and Lily felt a thrill of excitement as they dashed after her.

Goldie ran towards a bare, lifeless tree in the middle of the meadow, and it suddenly burst into life. Tiny green leaves unfurled and a carpet of primroses and violets flowered in the grass below. A pair of rooks chattered in the topmost branches, and a baby woodpecker peeped out from a hole in the trunk.

Goldie touched her paw to the tree and words appeared in the bark. Jess and Lily read them aloud.

"Friend...ship... For...est!"

A door appeared in the trunk. Jess glanced excitedly at Lily and turned the leaf-shaped handle. The door opened, spilling out golden light.

Goldie leapt inside and the girls followed. As they entered the golden glow, they tingled all over. They knew that tingle meant they were shrinking, just a little. Lily squeezed Jess's hand, wondering what adventure they were about to have!

As the light faded, the girls found themselves in a sun-dappled forest glade. Clumps of tangling violets scented the air, and there was Goldie, standing upright and wearing her glittery scarf.

"Jess! Lily!" she cried, hugging them. "I'm so happy to see you!"

"And we're happy we can talk to you at last!" Jess said.

"Is everything OK?" asked Lily.

"I'm not sure," said Goldie. "Someone needs your help."

She unfolded a letter. "Hermia the butterfly brought me this flyer from Ranger Tuftybeard the goat," she said. "He lives on Magic Mountain, beyond Friendship Forest. Here, read his letter."

Jess took it and read aloud.

"*Dear Goldie,*

Grizelda's been up to her old tricks again. She's threatened the families who live on the mountain, saying she's going to stop magic being made there. 'Tis bad news.

I heard tell that two girls helped you defeat

 18

Grizelda. Will they help us? Hope to see you soon.

Ranger Tuftybeard."

Lily and Jess exchanged worried looks. "That's definitely bad news," said Lily.

Grizelda was always making horrible plans to force the animals to leave

 19

Friendship Forest, so she could have it
all to herself. So far, Goldie and the girls
had managed to stop her every time, but
Grizelda would never give up.

"Will you help the ranger stop the
mean witch?" Goldie asked the girls.

Jess and Lily nodded eagerly. This
looked like the start of a new adventure.

"Of course we will!"

CHAPTER TWO

The Train to Magic Mountain

"Magic Mountain!" said Lily. "That sounds exciting!"

"It must be far away if it's beyond the forest," said Jess. "How will we get there?"

Goldie's green eyes twinkled. "You'll see," she said. "Follow me." She led them

 21

along a straight avenue of tall poplar
trees, towards a low hill.

As they rounded the hill, the girls stared,
astonished, at a small green and yellow
cabin. Stretching away on either side were
railway tracks. A sign said "Forest Halt."

"A train station!" Jess cried in delight.
"We never knew Friendship Forest had a
railway!"

Choo! Choo! Choo!

"A train's coming," Lily said.

Goldie smiled. "It's our train!"

The girls stared at her, thrilled, then turned to watch a tomato-red engine with a gold stripe approach the station. Behind was a matching carriage. The engine's tall funnel puffed clouds of pink steam.

The chuffing stopped, the train slowed to a halt and the driver leaned out. He was a pug dog, wearing a huge pair of goggles. His cap badge said "Driver" in shiny gold letters.

"Morning!" he said. "I'm Mr Whistlenose, and I'm your driver for today. All aboard for Magic Mountain!"

"Thanks, Mr Whistlenose!" the girls called, and climbed into the carriage behind Goldie.

They sat on comfortable green and gold seats. Between them a table held

a plate of watercress biscuits, a jug of pineapple fizz and three little china cups.

Goldie and the girls munched happily as the train chuffed through the forest.

Peep! went the engine's whistle as they passed Pat Shinyshell the tortoise on one of his long, slow forest walks. They all waved. Just as Pat was going out of sight, he waved back. Then there was another *peep!* The Dappletrot Shetland ponies were cantering alongside their carriage.

"Yoo hoo!" yelled little Maisie Dappletrot as the girls waved.

The track curved around a bend, and

a pink puff of steam bobbed by the open window.

"The steam looks like candy floss," said Lily.

"Like you could eat it," added Jess.

"Why don't you try some?" Goldie reached out of the window and caught some in her paw.

Lily sniffed the puff. "It smells like candyfloss too!" she said, and tasted it. "It *is* candyfloss! Yum!"

Goldie pointed ahead to a tall mountain. Its lower slopes were lush and green, while the upper half was

covered with shimmering ice and surrounded by fluffy clouds. "That's Magic Mountain," she said.

"It's beautiful," Lily said. "This is so exciting!"

A short while later, the train pulled into a station near the foot of the mountain. On the platform stood a big white goat with a neatly combed beard. He wore a knitted waistcoat, a backpack and a cowboy hat with holes for his horns.

He stepped forward and greeted the girls. "Howdy do! I'm Ranger Tuftybeard, and you must be Lily and Jess. I'm so glad you've come."

"We're pleased to meet you," said Jess.

"We hope we can help," Lily added.

Peeep! The train was pulling away. They waved goodbye to Mr Whistlenose, then headed towards Magic Mountain.

"I hope you can help too," said Ranger Tuftybeard. "'Twill be terrible if Grizelda causes trouble. And here's why." He opened his backpack and took out a glittering crystal.

"Wow! That's sparkly!" said Jess.

"Crystals like these," said Ranger Tuftybeard, "hold all the magic of Friendship Forest."

The girls stared in astonishment.

"What do you mean?" Lily asked.

"Have you ever wondered how Friendship Forest gets its magic?" asked

Ranger Tuftybeard as they walked.

The girls looked at one another, wide-eyed, and giggled. "Well, actually, no!"

Goldie chuckled. "How funny! I never thought to explain it to you before. The process of making magic is very complicated and very special. It has to be done just right. Only four families know exactly how to turn these crystals into magic. Ranger Tuftybeard's job is to carry the crystals between them."

Lily and Jess couldn't believe what they were hearing.

"How does it work?" asked Jess.

"There are four steps to making the magic, each as wonderful as the next. First the crystals are dug carefully out of the mountain," said the goat. "Then they're tended to and grown with love. After that, they're made into a magical mixture. Then – finally – when the mixture is just right, it's turned into clouds."

 31

"Why clouds?" asked Lily.

"The clouds rain down over Friendship Forest," said Ranger Tuftybeard. "They cover the whole forest with magic!"

"Then the crystals must be really important," said Jess.

"Really, really important," said the goat, as Goldie nodded in agreement.

The girls exchanged a worried glance.

"So," Lily began as they reached the foot of the mountain, "if Grizelda harms the mountain, she'll destroy the magic in Friendship Forest?"

"Exactly so," said Ranger Tuftybeard.

"Now, let's go and meet the first of the four families – the family that mines the crystals."

He showed them to an archway of gleaming silvery stone. "That leads to the Hoppytail family's mine."

Suddenly, lots of fluffy rabbits bounded through the arch – two adult rabbits and twelve young ones.

"Hello!" they cried.

"We're Mr and Mrs Hoppytail," said a rabbit in a blue cardigan. "And these are our children!"

The girls kneeled down and the

adorable little bunnies scrambled all over them, smiling and saying hello. They each clutched pawfuls of twinkling crystals of all different colours that they wanted the girls to see.

Ranger Tuftybeard introduced Goldie, Jess and Lily. "They've come to help us stop Grizelda," he explained.

"Thank you!" Mr Hoppytail said to Lily and Jess. Then he told the little bunnies to put their crystals in Ranger Tuftybeard's backpack. "Pippa, you're the oldest. You first," he said to a dainty little bunny with pale grey fur and a white

tail like a fluffy pompom. She wore a
necklace in the shape of a heart.

Pippa handed
over her crystals
to the ranger.
"Shall I show you
how we get the
crystals out of the
mountain?" she
asked the girls.

"Yes, please,
Pippa," said Jess.

Mr Hoppytail handed Pippa a hammer.
The hammer glittered and flashed in the

sunlight.

"Wow! That's even more sparkly than the crystals!" said Lily.

"It's made out of diamond," Pippa said. "It's the magical hammer we use to chip out the crystals from the rock."

Suddenly Lily gasped and pointed. A yellow-green orb of light was floating towards them.

"Oh no!" cried Jess. "Look out, everyone!"

The orb burst in a shower of smelly sparks. There stood Grizelda the witch, with her green hair whipping around her

 37

bony face. She swished her cloak over her

purple tunic and skinny black trousers

and cackled. "Ha-haa! I've got you now!"

CHAPTER THREE

The Purple Cavern

"Leave Magic Mountain alone,
Grizelda!" Goldie shouted.

"Mind your own business, cat!" the
witch snapped. "And you interfering girls
needn't think you'll stop my plan to take
over Friendship Forest this time. It's much
too brilliant for you!"

 39

She turned towards four rugged rocks nearby.

"Here, you!" Grizelda snapped.

Jess and Lily could hardly believe their eyes as the rocks quaked, uncurled and transformed into four grey creatures with wrinkled leathery skin and goggly eyes.

"Trolls!" cried Mr

Hoppytail, bounding in front of his children. "Stay back, little ones!"

"Meet my new servants," said Grizelda. "Rocky!"

A troll with shaggy grey hair and a stubby nose shambled forward. "Yerss," he said.

"Flinty!" said Grizelda.

"Yeah," said a troll with sticking-out ears. She grinned, showing gappy teeth.

"Craggy!"

"Eh?" Craggy had spiky white hair. He shuffled forward on knobbly grey feet.

"Pebble!" said Grizelda.

"What?" Pebble had extremely long arms and a long, wobbly nose, which she wiped with the back of her hairy hand.

Grizelda tossed lumpy cakes to the trolls. "Have some Nutty Snacks!"

"Om-nom-nom!" they yelled, diving to grab and gobble the snacks.

Grizelda cackled again. "I'll get rid of

all the horrid sparkly magic, then there'll only be witchy magic – for ever!" she shrieked. "The animals will have to leave the forest and it will be mine. All I have to do is … this!"

She pointed a bony finger, shooting

sparks at the diamond hammer, which Pippa was holding tightly in her paws. The hammer started to

move. The Hoppytails squeaked in horror
as Pippa struggled to hold on to it. The
hammer wriggled free and flew straight
into Pebble's hairy hand.

"No! Give it back!" Pippa squealed.

The little Hoppytails burst into tears
and huddled together in a bundle of fluffy
white tails. Lily bent down and hugged
Pippa. "We'll get it back!" she said.

"You won't," Grizelda cackled. "I
haven't finished! Trolls! You greedy
guzzlers will keep that hammer away
from the meddling girls and the silly cat,
won't you?"

"Yerss."

"Yeah."

"Eh?"

"What?"

Grizelda smiled her mean smile. "In return, you'll get the biggest feast you've ever seen!"

"Om-nom-nom!" yelled the trolls.

"GO!" screeched Grizelda.

She clapped her hands and the trolls were whisked off their feet, as if in a strong wind. With a *whoosh*, they flew into the mine at top speed, disappearing in the velvety darkness.

"You'll never catch them now,"
Grizelda smirked. Then she snapped her
fingers and disappeared in a spatter of
smelly sparks.

Ranger Tuftybeard comforted Mr and
Mrs Hoppytail, who were too
shocked to speak. Goldie and
the girls cuddled the upset
little Hoppytails.

Pippa
covered her
face with her
tiny paws.

"With the hammer gone, we can't collect the crystals we need to make magic for the forest!" she sobbed.

Lily stared at Jess in dismay. "We must get it back," she said. "Without magic, there'll be no food on the Treasure Tree for the animals, no flowers to make medicines ..."

Jess gulped. "And no Friendship Tree! We'd never be able to visit the forest again!"

Goldie mewed, her eyes full of tears. "I'll never let that happen! I'll stop Grizelda somehow."

 47

"We all will," Jess said firmly. "First we have to find that hammer." She gave Pippa an extra-large hug.

"The trolls went inside the mine," said Lily. "We'll start there."

"I must climb the mountain and deliver what crystals we have," said Ranger Tuftybeard. "These crystals will make us some magic, but they will run out eventually. We'll keep making it until they do." He hoisted his bag on to his back. "But you won't have much time, I'm afraid."

"We'll do our best," said Jess. They

 48

waved goodbye and watched him hop nimbly up a steep mountain path.

"You're going to need some help to get the hammer back," said Mrs Hoppytail. "Pippa, what about your special collection?"

Pippa's eyes sparkled. "That's a great idea! Follow me, you three!" She took the girls and Goldie into the mine. The tunnel was lit by glow-worm lanterns. Soon they reached a huge cavern with shimmering purple rock walls that glittered in the flickering light. Other tunnels led in different directions.

Pippa showed them the crystals
embedded in the shimmering wall.
"These are what we collect," she said.

Lily looked puzzled. "But there are
thousands!" she said. "Why can't we just
use these to
make magic?"

"We can't
get them
out of the
wall without
the magic
hammer,"
Pippa

explained. She picked up a fallen stone and chipped at a sparkling crystal. It stayed firmly stuck in the wall. "We have other hammers, but none of them will work without the magic one. That's why we must get that hammer back."

Pippa led the girls through a narrow gap into a smaller cavern. "This is our home," she said.

The stone walls were painted bright blue and orange and the polished floor glittered in the light of dozens of tiny glow-worm lanterns. A pot of carrot and onion soup simmered on the stove.

"It's lovely and cosy," said Jess.

They passed a small cave where the six boy bunnies slept. A teeny, tiny teddy sat on each blue bedspread, and six white cupboards stood against the wall.

Then they saw the girls' room, which had six beds with frilled lilac bedspreads and six yellow cupboards. "It's so pretty!" said Lily.

Pippa opened a cupboard with her name painted on it in blue. Inside was a huge silver ornament, shaped like a many-petalled flower. It sparkled and flashed in the lantern light with every

colour of the rainbow.

"That's gorgeous!" said Jess. "Can I hold it?"

"You can try," said Pippa.

Jess tried to lift it, then said, "That's too heavy!"

"It has magic powers that might help

 53

you, though!" said Pippa.

"Not if we can't carry it," Lily said sadly.

The bunny smiled and pulled a silver petal off the flower. As it came away, the girls saw it was attached to a silken

thread. It changed colour from silver to blue.

"This blue petal pendant is for you, Goldie," Pippa

said, hanging it around the cat's neck. It sparkled against her golden fur.

"Thanks, Pippa!" said Goldie.

"The pendant has a special power," said the bunny. "It can make things change colour."

She broke off a petal that became pink and put it around Jess's neck. "This one can transform things into something with a similar shape."

As Pippa hung a white petal around Lily's neck, she said, "This pendant can make things disappear!"

"Thanks!" said Lily. Her eyes shone

 55

as she gripped Jess's hand. "Magic!" she whispered. "Magic of our very own!"

CHAPTER FOUR

Boulder Trouble

Jess was puzzled. "How do our pendants work?"

Pippa smiled. "You hold it, concentrate, and say the magic words: 'Crystal flower, show your power!' But," she warned, "the magic only lasts a short while." She closed the cupboard and gave a brave little smile.

 57

"I want to come with you, but I don't think Mum and Dad would let me. I just hope the pendants will keep you safe while you're looking for the trolls."

Lily hugged her. "Thanks, Pippa."

Mr and Mrs Hoppytail came to say goodbye.

"I wish we could come," said Mrs Hoppytail, "but we've so many little ones to look after and we can't leave them whilst Grizelda is lurking around. I can give you something, though." She hurried to her larder, and returned with a little basket. "Freshly baked rock cakes," she

 58

said, handing the
basket to Lily. "All
buttery and full of
sultanas!"

"Don't get lost
in the tunnels,"
Mr Hoppytail
said, his nose
quivering with worry.

Pippa hopped around him. "If I went,
too, they'd never get lost! I know the
tunnels well, and I'd be so useful."

Mr Hoppytail took her paws in his.
"You can go, if you promise to be

 59

careful," he said. "Grizelda is dangerous."

"I promise," said Pippa, clasping her little paws.

"We'll look after her," Lily added.

The four friends said goodbye to the Hoppytails, and set off down a long twisty tunnel. Glow-worm lanterns hung from the roof, showing the way with a warm light.

"Keep a lookout for clues that can tell

us which way the trolls went," Goldie whispered.

The girls followed Pippa's white tail, wondering what was coming next.

After a while, Lily said, "There's not a sound from the trolls. Maybe they went down a different tunnel. Let's go back and start again."

Pippa's nose twitched. "I think we should keep going," she said. "There's a

weird smell down here. It smells icky and dirty."

"Like trolls!" cried Jess.

They carried on, faster now, and soon the tunnel widened out and split into two.

"Which way now?" wondered Goldie.

"Ah-choo!"

They looked around, startled.

"Bless you, Lily," said Jess.

"It wasn't me," said Lily.

Goldie shrugged and Pippa shook her head.

"Then who was it?" asked Jess.

The others looked confused.

 62

"It sounded really close," Pippa said nervously. Jess looked around, then peered closely at a large rock standing where the tunnel divided.

"This rock's not the same colour as the rest," she said. She stuck out a finger and poked it.

"Ouch!" said the rock. It quaked, uncurled and turned into a troll with

spiky white hair and knobbly grey toes.

Jess leapt back. "Craggy!"

"Ah-choo!" went the troll. "Bunny make me sneeze. Craggy go."

He lumbered down the left-hand tunnel.

"After him!" cried Lily. "He'll lead us to the others – and the hammer."

They followed Craggy along the short tunnel towards another cavern. But before they could reach the end, the troll shoved a huge boulder

into their path, blocking their way.

"He's getting away!" said Goldie, pushing at the boulder.

They all pushed and pushed, but the boulder would not budge.

"What are we going to do?" Jess grunted, shoving as hard as possible.

"The pendants!" said Pippa. "Maybe one of them can help!"

The friends looked down at their crystal petals.

"Mine makes things disappear, doesn't it, Pippa?"

said Lily. "I'll use it on the boulder."

The bunny looked doubtful. "I don't think the magic's strong enough to send away something that big," she said. "You could try – but concentrate really hard."

Lily held her pendant near the boulder and said firmly, "Crystal flower, show your power!"

The boulder shimmered slightly.

"You're right, Pippa," said Lily, disappointed. "It's not strong enough."

"Maybe if we all concentrate …" Jess said hopefully.

Everyone concentrated as hard as they

could, as Lily said, "Crystal flower, show your power!"

This time, the boulder shimmered a little, then a little more, until the whole thing looked slightly see-through. Then it vanished.

Four faces lit up.

 67

"That pendant's brilliant!" said Jess. "Thanks, Pippa!"

Pippa couldn't stop smiling. "It's been in the Hoppytail family for years!"

"Let's hurry," said Goldie, "before the magic wears off."

They dashed into the next cavern.

"Everybody tiptoe," said Jess. "If we're going to find that hammer, we have to listen out for the trolls!"

CHAPTER FIVE

Stalagmites and Stalactites

The four friends crept across the cavern.
At the other side, they saw that the tunnel
split into three.

"Oh!" said Goldie. "Which way now?"

"Listen!" said Pippa.

A rumbling sound came from deep in

the centre tunnel.

"Is it an earthquake?" cried Lily.

"It can't be," said Jess. "The ground's not moving. It must be a rockfall."

But the rumbling continued. "It can't be a rock fall," said Goldie.

Jess entered the tunnel and stood still, listening.

"It's not an earthquake or a rockfall," she said. "It's laughter!"

Lily listened, too, and heard rasping, rumbling sounds. "It could be laughter," she said.

"It's troll laughter," Pippa said,

bouncing excitedly. "If we follow the sound, it will lead us to them, and to the magic hammer!"

They all crept along the tunnel. But instead of finding four laughing trolls, they found a dead end – a wall of rock.

"They've blocked our way again!" cried Jess.

The friends flopped down on the ground in disappointment. Pippa climbed on to Jess's lap for a comforting cuddle.

Lily fingered her pendant. "This magic wouldn't be strong enough to make a whole wall disappear," she said. "We'll

71

have to go back."

"We've come so far," said Jess. "And Ranger Tuftybeard said we didn't have much time!"

"I've thought of something!" said Pippa. She reached up to touch Jess's pendant. "You can use this to change an object into something else – something the same shape."

"Like what?" asked Goldie.

Pippa smiled. "Something we can use to chip at that wall of rock. We could make a hole!"

Jess dropped a kiss on Pippa's head.

"Clever bunny!" she said. "Let's try."

The others moved closer, and Pippa jumped down. "Start with an object that's the right shape," she said Pippa.

"OK," said Lily. "Let's see what we've got."

Jess emptied her pockets. There were the little sketchbook, pencil and rubber she always carried. All Lily had was a

 73

hairslide and the basket of rock cakes.
Goldie put her scarf on the pile and Pippa
added her heart necklace.

"Hmm, I suppose the scarf and
sketchbook could make the shape of a
spade," Lily suggested.

Jess moved things
around, trying
to get ideas.
Suddenly she
grabbed her
pencil. "Look!"
she cried.

"This is long

and thin, like a handle, right? If I put the rubber on top, it looks like a hammer!"

"A hammer's perfect for breaking up rock!" said Pippa, bouncing in a circle. "Say the words, Jess."

Jess grasped her pendant, concentrating hard on what she wanted. "Crystal flower, show your power!"

With a shimmer, the pencil and rubber transformed into a hammer.

Pippa grabbed it and began chipping at the rock wall. "I must be quick!" she said. "The magic won't last."

The girls and Goldie watched, amazed,

 75

as Pippa's paw flew backwards and forwards so fast it was a blur.

"Wow!" said Lily. "That's incredible!"

Chunks of rock fell to the ground and a small hole appeared in the wall.

"I can hear the trolls better now," said Jess. "They're not far away!"

Soon the hole was big enough for a rabbit to crawl through. Minutes later it was big enough for Goldie and the girls.

"Oh!" Pippa said, looking startled. She held up the pencil. "The hammer's changed back already. We made that hole just in time."

"You did, you mean," said Jess, taking
her pencil. She picked up the rubber from
where it had fallen to the ground and put
it safely in her pocket.

The four friends crawled through the
hole into a vast cavern. Long sharp rocks

hung from the ceiling, and others pointed

upwards from the ground.

"It's like a stone forest!" said Lily.

"The hanging ones are called

stalactites," said Pippa. "The standing ones

are stalagmites."

"You certainly know about rocks and stones!" said Jess.

"Mum and Dad teach me," said Pippa. "I love learning about them."

They wiggled through the stalagmites towards the sound of the trolls.

Suddenly Lily put out an arm.

"Stop!" she whispered. "They're just ahead. This might be our only chance to get the hammer!"

CHAPTER SIX

Crumbs!

The friends crept nearer and hid behind a thick stalagmite. The trolls were sitting in a circle, eating something crunchy.

Lily grinned. "They're having a picnic!" she whispered.

Crumbs exploded all over the place as the trolls crunched and spluttered.

 81

Rocky and Craggy fought over a big pointy-topped cake. "Give me volcano bun," rumbled Craggy.

"No! Mine!" said Rocky. He snatched the bun and bit into it. Red jam squirted from the top, all over his stubby nose.

Lily nudged Jess and pointed to where the hammer lay between the trolls.

But Jess couldn't quite see. She stepped forward and accidentally kicked a stone. It bounced towards Pebble, who turned and spotted them. "Girls!" she yelled. "Girls want hammer!"

Flinty grabbed it, and the trolls

82

lumbered to their feet and loped off,

deeper into the cavern.

"Come on!" cried Jess. "We can catch

them – we have to!"

Even though the trolls weren't fast

movers, they made their way with ease

between the sharp rocks. Pippa, being small, could easily nip in and out of them, but the cavern was huge and the trolls kept disappearing behind the rocks.

Jess ran to the right, then heard a noise to the left and whirled around, bumping into Lily.

They dashed this way and that, following the noises of the trolls' heavy footsteps and grunts. But they were always too late.

 84

"They're not fast, but they're good at dodging," puffed Pippa.

"You're right," said Goldie, leaning against a rock. "We'll never get the hammer back like this. We need a plan."

Lily noticed something on the ground. "Crisp crumbs!" she said. "We must have circled back to where the trolls were having their picnic."

"We should keep going!" said Jess. "Maybe we can still catch them!"

"Wait a second," said Lily. "Do you remember how Grizelda promised the trolls a feast as a reward for helping her?"

"That's right," said Jess.

Lily waved the basket of rock cakes that Mrs Hoppytail had given them. "Maybe we can use these to get the hammer back." She frowned. "I'm not sure how …"

"We could lure them away with a trail of crumbs," said Jess.

"But they'd take the hammer with them," said Goldie.

Pippa bounced in a circle again. "Let's use the fake hammer to make them think they've got the wrong one. If they think ours is the real one, maybe we can trick

them into leaving the real one behind."

"That won't work," said Jess, patting her pocket. "The hammer's already turned back into my pencil and rubber."

Pippa bounced even more. "Try to use your pendant again!"

Jess's face brightened. "Can I?" She put the pencil down and set the rubber at the end, making a hammer shape. Then she held her pendant, concentrated, and said, "Crystal flower, show your power!"

The pencil and rubber shimmered and transformed into a hammer once more.

"Wait, I can use my pendant to change

the colour," said Goldie. "Crystal flower, show your power!"

This time, when the shimmering stopped, the friends gasped. The hammer was beautiful, although not anywhere near as glittery as the real hammer.

Jess placed the hammer on top of a large flat stone. "We have to try."

They each crumbled a rock cake, making a crumby trail across the cavern.

Then they hid behind a large boulder, as close to the hammer as they could get.

Lily hugged Pippa. "Let's hope this works," she whispered.

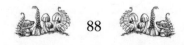

CHAPTER SEVEN

Tricking Trolls

Goldie, Pippa and the girls waited behind the big boulder. Moments later there was a delighted yell from across the cavern.

"Om-nom-nom!"

Jess grinned. "They've found our trail."

Lily giggled. "Listen to them!"

Guzzling noises echoed around the

cavern as the trolls gobbled pieces of cake.

Goldie peeped out. "They're getting

nearer. I can see knobbly toes."

"Oooh!" said Pebble. "Hammer!"

The girls peered out. The trolls had

gathered around the large flat stone.

"Better hammer!" said Flinty.

Rocky looked at the real hammer, then

grunted. "New hammer not as sparkly."

Craggy screwed up his face in

concentration. "But more stony! Better!"

The trolls frowned, as if they were thinking hard.

Lily and Jess held their breath. Would the trolls fall for the trick?

Craggy shook his head. "No," he said. "Trolls already got magic hammer. New one no good."

They watched the trolls lumber away.

"It didn't work!" whispered Pippa sadly.

"Wait," said Jess. "There's one last thing we can try." In a very loud whisper she said, "The trolls are so silly for thinking they've got the real magic hammer."

 91

Lily grinned. "Yes," she whispered. "They don't know Mr Hoppytail hid the real one in this cavern. We knew the trolls would fall for it and take the fake one."

"They think sparkly is better," said Goldie. "Aren't they silly?"

Jess added, "Yes, and it's easy to spot the real one. It's so much more stony!"

There was the scrabble of troll feet, then a voice said, "Trolls got wrong hammer!"

Lily peered around the boulder to see Rocky fling the real hammer aside and grab the fake one.

"Better hide hammer," he said.

They hurried away into the cavern.

The four friends rushed out from
behind the boulder, and Pippa picked up
the real diamond hammer.

She hopped around in delight. "We've
got it! Hooray!"

Goldie grinned. "Come on, " she said.
"Let's head home."

"This way," said

Pippa.

She led them

back

through

the tunnels.

When they reached the purple cavern, all the Hoppytails bounded over.

"Well done!" cried Mrs Hoppytail.

"We couldn't have found it without Pippa and her pendants," said Lily.

There was a low rumbling sound.

Jess and Lily looked at each other in alarm. Was it the trolls?

But Pippa didn't seem worried. "We used up the rock cakes. I'm starving. My tummy's growling like an angry troll!"

Mr Hoppytail laughed. "Come into the kitchen, then," he said. "There's lots to eat for everyone!"

CHAPTER EIGHT

Flower Power

Jess and Lily were enjoying the treats Mr and Mrs Hoppytail had set out on their long table.

The young Hoppytails' eyes nearly popped when their mum brought in a giant dish of iced cakes. "Honey bunny buns!" said Pippa. "Om-nom-nom!"

Everyone burst out laughing!

Mr Hoppytail played some tunes on his piano, and soon everyone was dancing.

Afterwards, while the little Hoppytails played Hide-and-Squeak, Pippa asked Jess and Lily, "Would you like to try the diamond hammer?"

"Ooh, yes!" they replied.

Pippa fetched the hammer, and took them to the purple wall. Jess had the first go. She'd barely touched the wall when a beautiful crystal popped into her hand.

"Wow!" she said. "Your turn, Lily!"

Lily chipped out a crystal, too. "It's as easy as cutting butter," she said.

Pippa grinned. "It's magic!"

Then a voice spoke from the cavern entrance.

"Well, bless my beard and horns!"

It was Ranger Tuftybeard. He clattered his hoofs on the cavern floor. "You got the

97

hammer back!" he said.

"With help from Pippa," said Lily.

"And from Mrs Hoppytail's rock cakes,"
added Jess, making everyone laugh.

Ranger Tuftybeard grinned. "I knew
you would do all you could to protect
Magic Mountain," he said. "Thank you!"

"We're glad we've saved the magic,"
said Lily.

"And we're very glad we can keep
coming back here," added Jess.

Lily looked serious. "I've an idea for
making sure Grizelda and the trolls can't
find the hammer again. Goldie, can I

borrow your pendant?"

Pippa touched Lily's hand. "The magic doesn't last, remember?"

"Oh no! I forgot!" said Lily. She felt so disappointed. "Now my idea won't work."

The little bunny bounced happily. "You've forgotten something else!" she said. "The pendant's magic comes from the big silver flower. Come on!"

Everyone followed Pippa into the girl bunnies' bedroom. She opened her cupboard to reveal the silver flower. "Lily, say the magic words, and concentrate hard on what you want."

Lily held the magical hammer before the flower, concentrated, then said, "Crystal flower, show your power!"

The hammer quivered, then turned a rich shimmering purple, exactly the same colour as the cavern wall.

"Camouflage! That's brilliant!" said Jess, as the Hoppytails cheered. "Grizelda and the trolls won't be able to find the hammer now!"

After a hilarious game of Pin the Nose on the Troll, it was time for the girls to go. All the Hoppytails hugged them. Pippa was last of all.

"Keep your pendants," she said. "You might need them again."

"Thanks, Pippa," Goldie, Jess and Lily said together. They waved goodbye and followed Ranger Tuftybeard back to the station.

The train pulled in just as they arrived. Mr Whistlenose gave a friendly wave and a whistle. *Peeep!*

Goldie and the girls climbed aboard.

"Watch out for Grizelda, Ranger Tuftybeard," said Jess. "Goodbye!"

"Bye!" Goldie and Lily called as the train chuffed away.

They travelled to the forest station, thinking about their adventure with the Hoppytails. Then they walked back to the Friendship Tree.

"Goldie, you must fetch us at the first sign of trouble from Grizelda," said Lily.

Goldie took their hands in her paws. "I promise I will," she said. "We animals couldn't let Grizelda stop you from coming back to Friendship Forest."

She touched the Friendship Tree, and a door appeared in the trunk. The girls hugged her, then stepped inside, into golden light. They tingled all over as they returned to their proper size.

When the glow faded they were back in Brightley Meadow.

On the way back to Helping Paw, Lily gasped and pointed to a bowl of lettuce they'd left on the grass nearby.

The escaped rabbits were hopping around it!

Jess laughed. "They look fit enough to go back to the wild!" she said. "No

wonder they managed to dig a tunnel!"

The girls shared a smile. They knew another hoppy rabbit who was excellent at digging tunnels too!

The End

Wicked witch Grizelda is still trying to ruin the magic of Friendship Forest. Can little chipmunk Lola Fluffywhiskers help save the day?

Find out in Lily and Jess's next adventure,

Lola Fluffywhiskers Pops Up

Turn over for a sneak peek ...

"It's a perfect day for working outside!" said Lily Hart to her best friend Jess Forester. Her breath made little clouds in the crisp air as she raked the autumn leaves into a pile.

Jess pushed her blonde curls out of her eyes. "And working at Helping Paw is the perfect way to spend an afternoon."

Lily's parents ran the Helping Paw Wildlife Hospital from a converted barn at the bottom of their garden. Lily and Jess loved helping out whenever they could.

Mr and Mrs Hart were inside the

barn at this very moment, tending to the poorly creatures. Lily and Jess were clearing the paths between the outside runs.

Jess peered into a pen where a mother rabbit and her fluffy babies were busy crunching on carrots. Then she swept the path in front of the aviary, a glass birdhouse full of chirping robins and swallows.

As Lily added some more leaves to the growing heap they had gathered, there was a rustling sound and some of the leaves tumbled from the pile.

"That's strange," she said. "It's not windy today."

She was just peering down to investigate the pile of leaves when she saw something out of the corner of her eye.

A cat with golden fur and sparkling green eyes was running towards them.

"Goldie!" gasped Lily in delight.

That could only mean one thing.

"We're going to Friendship Forest!" exclaimed Jess.

Read

Lola Fluffywhiskers Pops Up

to find out what happens next!

Magic
Animal Friends

Can Jess and Lily save the magic of
Friendship Forest from Grizelda?
Read all of series six to find out!

COMING SOON!
Look out for
Jess and Lily's
next adventure:
Anna Fluffyfoot Goes for Gold!

3 stories in 1!

www.magicanimalfriends.com

Jess and Lily's Animal Facts

Lily and Jess love lots of different animals –
both in Friendship Forest
and in the real world.

Here are their top facts about

RABBITS

like Pippa Hoppytail:

- Rabbits are mammals and more than half the earth's population is found in North America.

- Female rabbits are called does, male rabbits are called bucks and baby rabbits are called kits.

- Rabbits can jump high and far because they have very strong back legs. They can reach up to one metre in height and three meters in length.

- When rabbits skitter around in all directions it is called a 'binky' and is an expression of joy.

Can you keep the secret?

There's lots of fun for everyone at
www.magicanimalfriends.com

Play games and explore the secret world of
Friendship Forest, where animals can talk!

Join the
Magic Animal Friends Club!

–✕ Special competitions –✕

–✕ Exclusive content –✕

–✕ All the latest Magic Animal Friends news! –✕

To join the Club, simply go to

www.magicanimalfriends.com/join-our-club/